Those Powerful

Moustaches Jhumkas and Poor me!!!

Those Powerful Moustaches Jhumkas

and Poor me!!!

Author

Shakti Dwesar Sharma

Published Internationally by

Pendown Press

Powered by G Gullybaba

PENDOWN PRESS

Powered by **Gullybaba Publishing House Pvt. Ltd.,**
An ISO 9001 & ISO 14001 Certified Co.,
Regd. Office: 2525/193, 1st Floor, Onkar Nagar-A, Tri Nagar,
Delhi-110035
Ph.: 09350849407, 09312235086
E-mail: info@pendownpress.com
Branch Office: 1A/2A, 20, Hari Sadan, Ansari Road,
Daryaganj, New Delhi-110002
Ph.: 011-45794768
Website: PendownPress.com

First Edition: 2015

ISBN: 978-93-83921-68-3

Layout Design: Pendown Press Publishing

Dedicated to the youth

From my grandma

To me

From me to you

Form you

To

The next generation

Just keep it going....

Foreword

Generally we come across many incidents that leave an everlasting impact in our minds. The origin of this book is one of such episodes.

A small part of this book was narrated in a gathering, where I was to drop my grand maa and carry on with my own schedules. But some how I just couldn't leave that place when I heard everybody laughing .The narrator went on! I heard till the end which was about 10 minutes.

I was told that it was an ancient old concept that transcended down from generation unknown. This humourous concept is presented to you with my analytical study for over a decade.

I thoroughly enjoyed while writing and elaborating the critical analysis. I hope you too enjoy reading it and retaining the message therein.

Shakti Dwesar Sharma
March 2015

Acknowledgements

- I am truly grateful to my sons for typing this book time and again, staying awake at nights and missing out their social gatherings.
- I submit my gratitude to my family and friends for reading and re reading the manuscript for me.
- I really wish to give my note worthy thanks to Ms. Neha Khera for taking endless dictations.
- I thank Gullybaba Publishing House Pvt. Ltd. & its entire team for appriciating my work & bringing it to you.

Contents

MEET THE MAIN CHARACTERS

Mukhiya

SHANTI THE TRUE PICTURE

The Hero

Wait to see him endlessly.....

THE HAVELI

The Haveli stood tall like a monument at the far end of the village. The Mukhiya's room in the center was none less than a village court room with a huge veranda in front of it. There were large 20 rooms, 10 on each side exhibited the welcoming nature of the entire family. It was an ancient monument designed by the most popular architect, almost a century ago. Yet its shine and maintenance exhibited Mukhiya's taste and a desire to maintain the status. It had been a tradition for many generations that every generation had only one heir. Quite contrary to the belief of the village, each generation was satisfied with one son to carry on the legacy. The villagers generally believed that a minimum of 4-5 kids were necessary to survive each generation.

Mukhiya, the only one to inherit the Haveli form his ancestors stood like a tall and dynamic personality. The strength of his character and being shown on his face though there was a smile that was generally seen missing. A commanding and generous personality who was often found solving the problems of all those who approached him, maintaining his own dignity and command.

Shanti lived upto her name. Her beauty was none less than the depth of the blue seas. She stood like a devi with her pale skin glowing, her aquamarine eyes, calm expressions, majestic aura and smooth shining hair. Her charms were none less than that of a queen. Shanti was only ten when Mukhiya's late father had declared their marriage and knots to be tied a few years later. She was an object of desire for any man and so a most appropriate match for the tall and handsome Mukhiya, who was then seventeen. She belonged to Mukhiya's family as well. Living five villages away. Mukhiya often got her glimpse from a distance during his horse riding. Shanti as usual hid herself away and Mukhiya smiled.

2

All was going perfect besides an occasional hollowness that they both realised. It was truly occasional. Mukhiya being the head of the village had witnessed the trauma of the villagers with large families and their desperate desires to bring up their children anywhere above farming. They had spent their entire lives struggling with all such issues. It was only his mother who got worried and spent years in praying. Shanti did it too but always in silence.

The Haveli's silence was often disturbed by the chirping of birds, the pigeons in the veranda who gathered there for their food. The gardener and his family were given a room outside the Haveli. The cooks and the servants all moved around happily narrating stories and gossips of the villagers. Their kids were sent to primary schools for education and their expenses were borne by Mukhiya himself. On the far end of the "Haveli" his horses stood well polished and nourished in the stable by his people while the cow sheds were often visited by his mother and Shanti.

Thirteen years had passed away. The thought of adoption was considered at some point of time but finally given up.

Mukhiya and Shanti were contented with each other's company. After attending to the whole days court, looking after the development pattern of the village and solving land related disputes Mukhiya would enter his room where Shanti waited for him.

At 6:30 pm the dinner was served where the mother accompanied them towards the dining hall. She could seldom murmer her thoughts to Mukhiya. Later at 7:00 pm the couple visited the temple at the river bank across the Haveli. By 7:30 pm the day was called off. The servants went back to their quarters. The light of lamps were lowered and Shanti and Mukhiya occationally enjoyed the teakwood jhula under the moonlight. The fragrance of chameli perfumed the entire backyard where the jhula was placed.

The village Astrologer and Haqim were regular visitors of the mother. Last year the astrologer came in with shine in his eyes. The Haqim had accompanied him. Lengthy discussions among the mother, the Haqim and the astrologer went on for many days. Nobody had the right to enter her room without her order. The secret was kept hidden from the couple. Later an ayurvedic medicine was offered to Shanti for a week. She knew what it would have meant but posed no queries, kept no hopes and took it gently with some interrogations in her eyes.

It was when she missed out her monthly cycles for four consecutive months, that the dai maa was consulted. She is carrying!!! Exclaimed dai maa. That was the day!!! Shanti was pampered in all possible ways.

The huge Haveli that had been giving the impression of an emperor that believed in peace and tranquility, which was engulfed with a silence suddenly turned into ecstasy, today after 14 years it stood tall, shining and filled with enthusiasm, waiting for the celebration to begin.........

THE CELEBRATION

The lights were lit all over the Haveli. People rushing from one corner to the other, trying to make all arrangements ready by 7.30pm. It was 6.30pm already and nobody was appropriately dressed. "First get ready and then do the finishing bits". There came a feeble yet commanding voice of a wrinkled face that held a great importance.

Shanti had given birth after 14years of her marriage. Finally the richest family of the village had a heir. **Shanti** was dressed like a bride. She was made to sit with the newly born on a special Diwan in the middle of the grand veranda facing the entrance. Everybody dressed to their best. The countryside house was decorated with lights and petals of roses spread on the pathway right from the entrance to the diwan on which Shanti sat.

The main gate was decorated with red and golden drapes, topped with multicolour flower bouquets. Ittar was showered all around. The food and drinks were arranged at the far end of the huge veranda, on the left side of the Diwan while the dhol and the music were arranged on the right side.

Shanti sat like a proud lady, a bit nervous though. The thought that the child should not catch anybody's evil intent caused the nerves to wreck.

The child, yet not officially named, being called as 'Raja' had a thick layer of kajal in his eyes and black tika on his forehead. This was a common tradition followed in the village. It was believed that this protects the child from evil well-wishers. For this, lemon and green chillies were hidden amongst the floweral décor outside the main gate. The wrinkles on the face of grandma had enough experience. Raja was dressed none less than a Prince in heavy satin dress quite contrary to the weather! It was important for him to look good and kept warm the dress was chosen by his aunt. Next to grandma she held a great authority and command in the family. Shanti and Mukhiya had little to say in the presence of her cheerful authority today. It was 7.15 pm and light music filled the atmosphere. People had started walking in. The greetings had made a big noise. The grandma joined Shanti and Raja now on the grand Diwan. The drumbeats and the sounds of the trumpets got louder now. Hearing all this noise, Raja was a bit uncomfortable. His discomfort grew as the mother's attention shifted towards the guests. Grandma had only one duty..... To accept the gifts and keep them carefully. A red bag in her hand collected the cash, while the gifts went behind her on the huge Diwan. The aunt took the responsibility of welcoming the guests.

All the men stood outside the Haveli to welcome the men while the females stood on the opposite side inside the Haveli. This was the tradition of the village. Everybody was excited besides Raja, who was the only serious witness of the entire celebration.

The description of this huge grand celebration came from none other than the new born, who had just witnessed the dark, secure yet a warm womb where he alone was the king and now was exposed to bright lights and a huge crowd where he found his own identity too little.

Read on the humourous description of the entire celebration from the vision of this few days old, Raja- the king!

✦ ✦ ✦

LOOK WHO IS TALKING

Just a few days ago, I came out of a tight yet secure, dark yet not gloomy, protected yet not a demanding womb. I was told I'm born. Born as the first child of unknown faces called a family. I was puzzled to see so many huge figures around me and it seemed as though my coming out of that womb, that secure and undemanding habitat was being celebrated.

I lied in the arms of a weak yet radiant woman. Endless noise of drum beats and things called people surrounded me. I watched carefully. The things called people present there were trying their best to feel close to each other. Some by shaking hands and some by embracing each other. There was yet another type who patted each other's back and laughed for nothing. It looked as though each one was trying to beat their own loneliness by intruding into the loneliness of the other. Each one trying to feel complete and possessed with equally incomplete and unpossessed souls. Their outward smiles seemed fake to me. Their fake smiles and desires to feel possessed by one or the other made it very obvious that they had forgotten that they were born alone like me. This was the right moment for them to remember this truthful fact but maybe the path called life had transformed their thinking and behaviour.

As soon as the drum beats got louder some sour smell perfumed the air and they started rocking in a funny manner. They called it a dance. I could realise that these funny and meaningless movements were done to shake off the blues of meaningful survival. By now I too had started feeling blue so I also tried rocking in similar fashion but my rocking was restricted so I managed to rock my arms and feet a little. I was not given that sour smelling liquid as well. Looking at them I forgot that I was analysing. So I continued staring and forgot to analyse why I was born and so had they. The celebrations went on....

THE LESSER THE BETTER

Then out of the blues came a man full of cheer and bad odour "Son, in relation I am your paternal uncle", he said and kissed me, pinched my cheeks and walked away with a smile. "All right", I said to myself, I believe you, and remembered that uncle's relations mean kissing, pinching and walking away with a smile. The lesser the better. The Kiss had shown emotions and the pinch had hurted me. Therefore, uncle's in relations meant giving me emotions, hurting and walking away with a smile. But the next apparent man called uncle came and introduced himself similarly. Yet there was a difference. He gently blessed my head, did not pinch my cheeks and walk away. This gentle blessing was soothing, exhibiting less of emotions for himself and full of care for me. Such uncles could be good for my survival.

✦ ✦ ✦

AUNTS DON'T
INTRODUCE

Just while I was beginning to feel a little good about someone gentle, there came a lady who almost snatched me from the lady called the mother without even introducing herself. She took me amongst some ghastly looking people like herself. I cried looking at them while they smiled and tried to soothe me. My analysis- the ghastly looking women will always take me for granted and order me around without even introducing themselves. I continued crying while they went on with ohley ohley ohley and ooo la la la...!! Their strange language. I was sure even they didn't know what it means. My analysis- when things called people have nothing to say they will always use this language. Oh, I thought to my self, this is the first practical vocabulary which I needed to remember throughout my life. It could come in handy in many situations. Finally I was handed back to the lady called the mother. The ghastly lady had thought that I cried to go back to her while the truth was that I cried seeing her huge face covered with many shades of different colours. She soon got a red coloured box which had some glittering things called jewellery. She had got it as a gift simply because I had lost my secure womb. My analysis- ones loss equals other gain.

Now I stayed calm with the lady called the mother I saw yet another batch of the restless souls around me, there came yet an another figure. His eyes gleamed as he looked at me, rolling up his moustache and face unshaved he bent down to kiss me and said in a loud and proud voice "son, in relation I am your father". Then suddenly he picked me and flunk me up into the air. While it was a very strange experience for me, he handed me back to the weak and the radiant lady. I realised that the thing called father put me up in the air because probably he wanted to see me on the top. If at all I could not make it there I would be handed back to the hands of the weak and the radiant lady where I laid. While I was busy analysing, he bent down kissing me, his kissing had pricked my cheeks once again with his thorny beard. Ok maybe, I agreed with myself about his being my father.

In relations by now I knew there was a lot of hurt. Through kissing they exhibited emotions and therefore, it is the emotions that hurt and not the kiss. It also meant that emotions were thorny in nature, irrespective of who exhibited them. With all these well-meant emotional hurts I started crying....

✦ ✦ ✦

THE HUG

The lady in whose arms I laid thought I was hungry. She hugged me closer with a lot of warmth. Her hug was soothing but at the same time gripping at my being. She brought me much closer to her body, pampered my head gently and said, "Son in relation I'm your mother". OK, I believe you, if you say so, but I know nothing. This voice was different. Her gentle touches were also different. They sounded familiar to the time when I was in the womb. A bit confused I said "sorry I couldn't understand you much", I said to myself probably she sensed the confusion, and said "I'm going to look after you because I have given you a birth. I realised that the combination of the two worlds, the womb and this outer space was only this lady and so this is where I will continue to get undemanding support and security. Surprisingly her kisses also didn't prick. I looked carefully she had no moustache as well, so I could expect to get no pricky emotions from her. The only thing that was unique and a bit scary was her tight grip over my completeness.

She fed me and by feeding I had gathered a lot of energy and I wanted to play. But she patted me softly and gently, "go off to sleep my son", she commanded. Oh! I realised feeding means commanding. That means who so ever will feed will command. The nature of food may vary from food to shelter, from shelter to emotions, from emotions to belongings. But its true nature will never change. Feeding will always be followed by a command.

Thinking of all this and remembering the command, I slept quite obediently so but the drum beats only got louder and woke me up.....

✦✦✦

PUTTING UP AN ACT HELPS

This time I got up silently. Didn't cry or move much. Had I done that, I would have been patted off to sleep again. My analysis- one has to put on an act just to do what one wants. Acting could also help to avoid commanding behaviours. So I acted... Silently.

POWER PLAY

This I realised was the power of acting and continued staring. There came a few little figures and started playing with my hands and feet. Their touches were soft and I enjoyed it. Their cute little faces churpy laughter, naughty looks amused me. I started laughing with them. When I laughed a little, they laughed louder they were as amused as I was.

We were all happy and playing. My analysis – in order to have happy people around one needs to smile and laugh. Ok, this is something important to remember but what if I didn't? I reflected back and notice that until now I was only crying and I was always handed back to the lady called the mother. My analysis-continuous crying over any or many issues makes people run away.

But this laughter and playing could not last long enough. A strong lady came and took them all away. They did not want to leave me and nor did I. They were as powerless as me. I thought and started analysing that my little friends had gone away crying and looking back. By now I knew why do people cry. Whenever anybody feels too little or powerless in any given situation-they cry. If one is powerless, he would only look back and cry just like me and my friends. I kept staring at them and those hands that dragged them away. Those hands had a lot of power. I, then tried making a tight fist of my hands and checked my biceps. No power at all! I was sad and upset. My analysis- one has to grow up powerfully enough so as not to be dragged. Power could be in many forms. One could be mentally or physically powerful, financially or emotionally powerful, but powerful they must be. If power in any of these forms would be missing dragging would be unavoidable.

RUPEES 500/-

Ok, this is world, A world of difference, I thought and went off to sleep. And in this sleepy state another lady took me into her arms. She called me with different names, gave a piece of paper that read ₹500 and commanded me to wake up. Once again, feeding money was another command. I cried for sleep but she refused to understand. My analysis – Money means crying and sleepless nights. After a lot of efforts I put into crying I was handed back to the lady called the mother." Son, I can understand that you are feeling sleepy "and she took me to another room and patted me off to sleep.

✦ ✦ ✦

THE FASCINATION

Just then came another lady with a noisy little thing in her hand. I woke up crying but at the same time I was fascinated with that noisy little thing. I was confused whether I was feeling sleepy or fascinated. My analysis-fascination causes confusion. They neither allow you to sleep nor wake up.

But the fascination could not last long and I told the lady called mother, "I am sleepy". But Alas! by then she had shifted her understanding from me to that lady. That means mother's understanding can also shift for a while let aside others. She gently introduced me to her, but her gentleness had little meaning for me. In that sleepy state, I felt everything like a command. I was sleepy and confused. Fascination had caused the confusion. To me it meant that , it is only in the sleepy state of mind that one is fascinated or confused. My analysis- confusion means fascination or a semi sleepy state of mind. If I had thought with my eyes open I would have realised the good and bad of that toy (fascination) and known whether it was worth it to lose sleep and cry. It was tearing me apart that if I took anything from anybody, be it kisses, hugs, money or material, I would have to take command and lose sleep. After hours of crying I was patted off. After waking up I realised that one has to be persistent to get what one wants. Persistence means too much of hard work to fulfill a natural desire with firm belief in one self. Persistence for sleep meant crying for hours. In other words desires mean sleepless nights, the lesser the better. I got hugs that gave a tight grip over my being, while I was born to be free. Kisses are followed by painful pricks; when they were supposed to express only soothing emotions. That meant all soothing emotions had the equal strength of hurting.

+ + +

CHASE THE GAZE

Just as I was busy analysing I saw something strange. A figure much smaller than that of the father was looking at something and smiling. This smile was strange to me, it had something special. Looked as though it was saying something I chased his gaze and looked at the other end. There stood a figure much smaller than that of the mother's. She too had a smile on her face that was quite similiar to him. I continued staring, shifting my gaze from one to the other repeatedly. Why were they smiling at each other? I tried differentiating and realised that she had no beard, moustache and looked brighter while he had only beard, moustache all over his face and looked not so bright. Oh, it was the brightness on her face and a bushy smile on his that brought about the admiration. He brushed his hand through his hair while she lowered her eyelids. She looked sweeter than ever. Looking at them I too tried to brush my hand through my hair but nobody smiled.Then I tried to lower my eyelids to look sweeter but the figure called mother thought I was slept. My analysis- for someone to smile at me in that special way I have to wait to grow up to that height and age. My tiny and little hands could only be noticed by my mother. My analysis- for an exchange of smiles and special gestures at least two people are required one with beard and moustache and one without it. Further more it was important for the two to understand the meaning of all these similiar actions. I also realised that somebody similiar to my size and height could only give me that meaningful smile. Until then the oldies would only be my best company....

NO GAZE TO CHASE

Having looked at them and experimenting with myself, I looked all around just to see if I was alone. But to my rescue I was happy to see that I wasn't the only one whose gaze didn't get a smile. I saw a lot of things like them but they were not smiling in that special manner. I noticed carefully and tried differentiating. They were close to each other, walked together, some even ate together and laughed but not smiled like them. I realised that peculiar smile can come only from a distance. To me it meant that if things called people got too close to each other, the smile would disappear. That smile had a sense of mystery. But the closeness had got the mystery to vanish. I further analysed it is important not only to maintain a distance, a well meant space in relationships, it is equally important to have some mystery attached to each individual. A well meant space, I thought, was enough to create a mystery. I started looking around again and to my amusement I noticed two wrinkled faces- one from each gender. I was astonished! As astonished to see the similiar mysterious smiles on their faces. Surprisingly they too didn't have teeth in their mouth... Just like me. I wondered. The wrinkled face of someone like grand maa shone when the other wrinkled face like father smiled at her. How was it that they had no teeth like me but exchanged smiles and why were my smiles were not reciprocated. Probably the wrinkles made the difference. I touched my face. It was plane and smooth. Yes I was right. Since I had no wrinkles it was fair enough, I thought to myself and lay contented. But that smile and the difference between the ages kept me thinking. Then out of the blues came a figure like the mother and exclaimed "Maa, you are looking gorgeous in this saari and this new bindi. Oh! I realised it was her changed attire. The change might not have been a routine. Maybe, I thought to myself, she wore that bindi and the saari with red and golden border that brought about the charm on her face which in turn got her that smile despite the missing teeth. So by now I had summarised quite a lot. My analysis- To get that special smile three things are very important-

- Maintaining a meaningful and peaceful distance.
- Maintaining a sense of curiosity.
- Changed set of attires.

If these three things were maintained the smile could last until the teeth fell. I studied further and noticed that the wrinkled faces with smiles had come a long way and there would have been many ups and downs where many things like me would have come their way. I guess all these might have just been enough to create the necessary distance. Looking at that saree I checked myself. I was adequately dressed but my dress could not be as apparent because I was too close to the lady called the mother. I was clinging to her. So I guessed clinging to anybody physically, emotionally or mentally could also drive the smiles away.

While I was busy analysing the clinging, I shifted my gaze to the lady figure with wrinkles.

She had just got a compliment and was amused. The young lady held her hand and took her towards the flavouring stalls. I saw she groaned with pain when she got up. She then pointed towards the old man with wrinkles. The young lady rushed towards him to get him. He too groaned with pain as he got up and started walking towards her. The agony of their pains shown on their faces. Together they moved towards the stall. I started wondering. Their smiles seemed much closer than the young and bright faces all around. What was it that created that strong bonding? Was it the pain? Yes, I was right. Things called people got closer to each other and agreed more with each other when in pain. To me it meant that all those who experienced the same pain and sorrow stuck closer to each other. My analysis-

- Pain brings people closer.
- People who understands each others pains and gains stuck together.
- The quality of the pain or the gain described the desires of mutual understanding and the quality of the group.

This I could realise because I saw all the wrinkled faces with their white shiny hair and missing teeth sat together on one side. Probably because they all agreed with each other's pains. While the young, full of cheer clad together in one group. My little friends too made funny movements and stuck together. This got me thinking. The wrinkled face, the young and my little friends thought and behaved in totally different manners. What if they were clubbed together? Would their thinking and behaviour ever match? I wondered and realised that the grey were quite like me because neither the oldies could move by themselves neither could I. Nor did I have teeth neither did they. The disability was also common. Yup! That's the secret behind oldies getting along well with people like me. By now I had known that the things called people would be happiest with their own peers. But what about me? I thought pitting myself and then suddenly smiled. A lot of grey were there at my disposal! My face gleamed with joy....

THE POWERFUL TAIL

Now that I was satisfied about having friends and a lot of them to play with, I saw something that was strange. It was small, about the height of my friends. It definitely did not look like the things called people. They called it a puppy. This creature was very amusing. It made very funny movements every time somebody came closer to him. He jumped with joy and sheer excitement. Probably this was the reason that he was pampered by all. I looked more keenly now. It welcomed everybody in a special manner. It had something additional that wagged his tail at everybody irrespective of who he was. They called it a tail. His gestures through this powerful tail could be ignored by none. Suddenly I touched my back. I had no tail at all. I was sad and disappointed.

And then Suddenly one of my friends jumped on his precious tail. He barked loudly. On his barking everyone moved away. While he barked I noticed he had a tongue in his mouth quite similiar to the things called people. It was the tongue that had made the noise. The wonderful tail was speechless and so admired. To me it meant that if the tongue yells irrespective of whose it is, all would run away. My analysis- It is better to wag a tail than the tongue. But since things called people had no tails behind them their tongue had more responsibility attached to it. They would have to use their tongue alone for solving both the purposes. To me it seemed like an impossible task. But no, things called people could do it!!

I noticed it when all the things called people suddenly ran towards the entrance. There entered a late comer. He was clad in an expensive attire. The latecomer seemed very heavy. Not because of his belly but because of the number of people entering with him. They were all dressed in black with something heavy, black and brown in their hands.

All people present there ran towards him. They all looked like the jumping puppy to me. Absolutely like the puppy, they jumped with an equal amount of enthusiasm. A special sitting arrangement was made for him. I tried differentiating. The things called people showered him with flowers and garlands. The garlands came upto his face. On one hand he seemed very pleased while on the other he looked totally stuffed up. It looked as though a lot of people had put that neck band in his neck, just like the puppies owner had put in his puppies neck. Oh! Now I realised why was the puppy holding his tongue out. It was the band that forced it out. I could see that man wanting to hold his breath and pop out his tongue. But he couldn't. So he popped out all the garlands himself. As he sat down, I saw all the things called people surrounded him. I noticed more carefully now they stood with their hands folded and eyes gleaming with joy. I guessed this was the way in which the things called people wagged their tails. They had learnt their lessons well. Wagging tails was very important. But there should have been a limit to this. They further bent down on knees to touch his feet. To me it looked as though they were actually giving him a proof and were feeling sorry for not having a tail behind them and proving it too- Probably this was the way of greeting all. I again looked around nobody else was greeted in this manner. To me it meant that there was some greed attached to this kind of welcoming.

Now I began noticing the similarities and the differences between the things called people and the thing called the puppy. While the puppy could manage it all by simply wagging its tail, things called people had to do the following to match that powerful tail-

- Show excitement while meeting anybody, irrespective of the fact whether you like him or not.

41

- Use the hands for solving the tails purpose.

- Use the tongue only for uttering the sweet nothings or memorising old sweet memories even if the person might have tried to kill you in the past or may do so in the future.

- The puppy did it to all- why not you do it too.

- In case you feel like barking, do so at home. Barking publicly runs the public away from you and gives you a bad name.

- The puppy had a band in his neck so put a nice looking band in your own neck. It creates a strong everlasting bonding.

- If you are upset, show it.

- For someone to notice that you are sad your initial exhibition of excitement and then sitting back sadly would bring about much better results.

- Capture all the sweet memories in a little box. It is called the camera. You never know when the things may go bad and these snaps could come in handy.

- Since the tongue has a lot of responsibility to itself, keep it under check while showing disagreements. It is likely to slip at such times.

After proper analysis regarding all the goodness of the things called puppies and the things called people, I turned around and looked at the flavouring stalls. I was shocked to see what followed next. A lot of huge puppies had walked in and vere busy in licking away the round plates. Some people were holding sticks and hitting them, trying to throw them out. I wondered and looked for the difference between two types of puppies. The one with the band belonged to an invitee and so he too stood an invitation while the huge puppies came uninvited. I learnt two lessons from this-

- Never go anywhere uninvited.

- If you are a latecomer, never be so late that the uninvited puppies are your only followers.

THE SPEECHLESS TREE

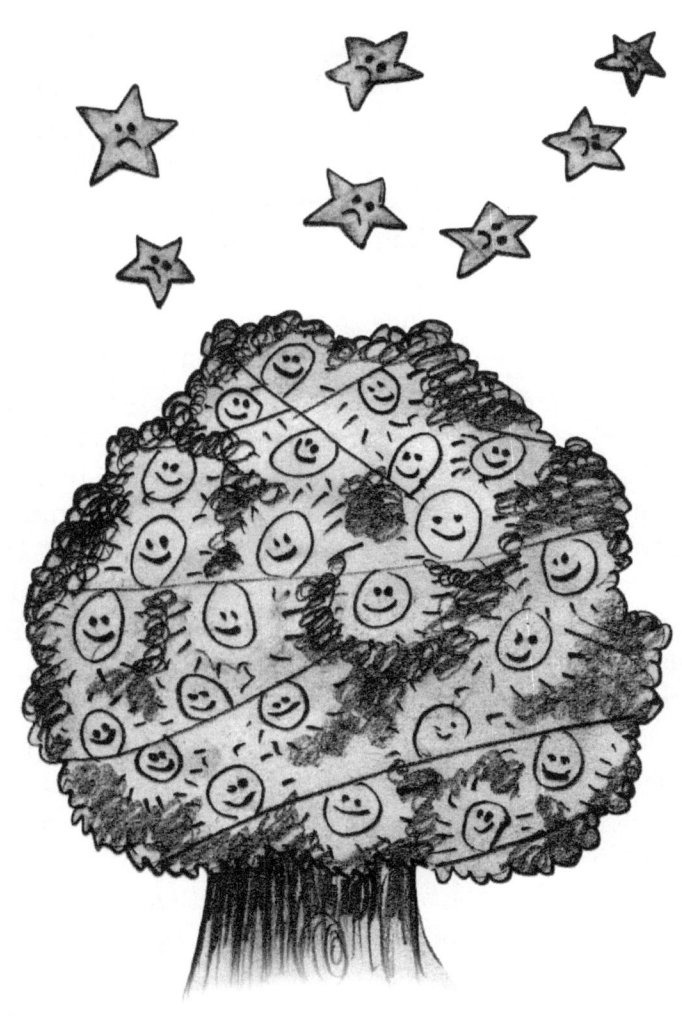

A s soon as the white man left without eating, the huge puppies who were busy eating were chased away, a lot of things called people started moving out.

To my relief, the drumbeats also stopped. It was beginning to feel peaceful. In this peaceful state, I saw many other things around me. Now that there was nothing much interesting to see around me, I looked up. I and the lady called the mother had been sitting on a Diwan which was placed under a huge thing that swayed. They called it a tree. The tree was heavily decorated with different colours of light that hurt my tiny and tender eyes a little. I looked still higher up. There was a black coloured sheet spread all over and had some small things shining gently at me. Looking at all this I realised many things. One, that one can actually see everything clearly only when they are at peace with in themselves. The vision became clearer and it became easier to differentiate. And so I started. I was told that, the black sheet above all of us was called the sky and the small little things smiling at me were called the twinkling stars. But somehow, the décor on the trees with artificial lights attracted people more than the soothing stars. For me it meant that, on this planet, artificiality attracts and helps in winning. So one had to put on artificial behaviours. It also meant that, howsoever successful the artificiality is, reality in its expression is as soothing as the light of the stars. To me it meant that, I would have to choose between the real smoothing smiles or artificial smiles to be successful in this world. It would be tough to be artificial all the time, I looked carefully again. To me it looked as if one had to be artificial only until they reached the top. Once they had reached there, they could enjoy the reality and gently share their smiles with all.

Later after sometime, the lights from the trees were removed. Oh! Now I realised, that the artificiality doesn't last for long. It can be unmasked at any point of time. The stars could not be removed by anyone. To me it meant that, if the things called people turned their artificiality to reality, or really being what they show, no one could pull them down like the stars. So I summed it down-

- Artificial behaviours can help only one to win.
- Artificiality can only be used as a tool to reach the top. It is the stepping stone towards the success.
- It stands a risk of being unfolded.
- One has to turn it into reality, so that no one can pull them down.
- Reality is ever lasting.
- The fact that, this is possible. It can be done.

THE UNSEEN

As I summed up, my study, I looked up at the tree once again. It was swinging freely now. The difference between the tree and the people was quite evident now. People swang only with the drums, then how was this tree swinging on its own? Probably it was happy that the burden was taken off from it. Alright, I realised, anything that had any kind of burden on itself cannot swing. Now I could correlate this to many things called people who did not swing with the drum beats. They might have been burdened with either inhibitions or with work or attitudes. "It is getting windy, bring Raja inside." Came a commanding voice. Wind! What was that? I tried searching it all around but could not see it. All the same, I could feel its chill. Now, this was altogether, a new ball game. What cannot be seen, can be definitely felt. And what can be felt, does manifest itself in some manner or the other. This also meant, that like the wind, feelings of the things called people, which cannot be seen can easily be felt by others. Just like the cool breeze was a manifestation of nature's happiness. So it was important for me to sum it so that, I don't forget it. So I summed it down:

- Every feeling can be felt.
- Feelings may not be exhibited but their manifestations are noticeable.
- When one is busy feeling, one cannot see the reality.
- One has to stop feeling and thinking to reach to the crux of reality.

✦✦✦

MOUTH THE LITTLE GATEWAY

Well I said to my self and starting look around. By now things called people had stopped dancing and went to the other side followed with the flavour of delicious dishes. Some big round like things were held in their hands and their mouth looked fuller even I was temped to join them but I realised that I had no strength at all and so the effects would be futile. I wanted to munch like them but satisfied my self by just lying there and copied their munching faces. My analysis- one needed strength- physical, emotional or financial to overcome dependence.

THE TODDLER

Just as I was busy pitting my self and huge figures were busy munching away, I noticed a small figure moving towards the garden. He moved on his knees and tiny little palms. I was fascinated. He crawled towards the garden and with one hand on the floor he picked up some thing with the other hand and put it in his mouth. Probably he too had watched everybody was munching away. So he too munched. Then out of the blues came a lady rushing towards him. She picked him up and forced the mud out of his mouth. He started crying. By now I had learned that this little mouth is one of the most important part of the body. It is only the mouth that seems to be the maintenance gateway of the human body and in order to sustain these huge figure a small little mouth was just enough. When I carefully noticed I saw that the mouth had something red in it. They called it a tongue. The tongue that swallowed anything and everything but at the same time made noise as well. I noticed it when the toddler started crying. His mother use the same tongue for yelling. They both kept using the tongue. One for crying and the other for yelling. Then came a wrinkled face using her tongue differentlyz. She took the toddler in her hands and uttered sweet sounding words. He stopped crying. Ok, I said to my self next to the mouth, the tongue was most important through which I could shout, yell, laugh and cry and uttered sweet little words at the same time.

The wrinkled face had the experience of the world. But only sweet words were not enough, the mouth still needed to work to munch. Only sweets words don't drive the hunger away. I noticed carefully the huge figures had got still hunger tummies that prompted out of their figures while toddler's tummy stuck to his backbone. Looking at their big tummies the toddler stated crying even louder. The tongue knew its functions very well. It knew exactly when to cry, laugh, yell or shut up. Now that he was crying, he was finally given a piece to munch. Probably he didn't like it. So he threw it down the wrinkled face seemed to be exhausted and sat down on the carpet near to my Diwan. The toddler once again escaped her gaze and crawled away as fast as he could. He again went back to the park and took some mud. I smiled with amusement. I was happy to know that a thing as little as him could fool the huge figures and wrinkled face. The huge figure were no less. He was caught again the mud was again taken out of his hand. My analysis-one I would always be denied at least one success in any given situation irrespective of how much hardwork had gone into it. It also meant that the success he so chased was not right for him. Had he chased something like all others, success would have been obtained. Alternatively he should be more smarter as doing hard work alone was not enough for achieving any success. Smart working was equally important to succeed.

I was happy with this analysis and went off to sleep.

THE DRAMA

When I woke up it was morning and half of the people had gone away. That half the exhibition of futile emotions were over. I then realised that I was crying throughout because I was analysing the situation too much. Had I stopped analysing, I would have enjoyed the evening throughout. Probably this is what makes the humans cry. Analysing every situation and every word, every figure, and their expressions take the peace away. Had I accepted every human as he/she was accepting in totality, the anguish would have been much lesser. Now I realised I was analysing no one else but myself. It couldn't continue for long. Self analysis never continues for long. It shifts to others very conveniently.

Just then, there came a figure called the father along with a wrinkled, exhausted little face with a bent over backbone, who he said was my grandmother. I saw her yesterday but she didn't look too attractive amongst all the young and beautiful faces. Even I ignored her presence. The lady called the mother, my mother told me that the grandma was my father's mother but I saw he no longer clung to her as I did.

Clinging to a mother was the first emotion of security that I had known. A few times, I saw similar kinds of tears in my mother's eyes when they were in my eyes too. She said the grandma was the purest form of love. Love? What was this? Was it agreeing in pain or in totality? What if there was a disagreement? Would it still be called love, I continued to wonder. Just then I saw the figure called the father arguing with the figure called the grandma and I realised that their love had faded out. He yelled while she sobbed and she yelled while he walked away. To me that meant that love is nothing else but an agreement over issues. Until yesterday evening, there was a love. Now there was an ego. Ego, tears, disagreements over the issues. Sometimes later the figure called the father came back and yelled at the lady called the mother who, until yesterday gleamed with joy and today sobbed with a gloomy face. The difference was once again the disagreement over the issues. The lady called the grandma came walking in, leaving behind her ego to say "do as you please". She had wanted to end the disagreement that means the power of the word or emotions called love had many aspects. One could call it love only if there was an agreement over all issues for a longer period of time and the ability of the opponent to let aside the ego which would determine the nature and strength of relations or a destiny of a relationship. If there was agreement issues over smaller number of issue, for a shorter period of time and the ego of the opponent was too high to surrender, we could call it indifference and no agreement at all over any issues be termed as hatred. To me that meant that there was nothing called love, hatred or indifference. But there certainly was either agreement or no agreement over the issues.

This was the end of the result of my all analysis of arguments between the figure called the father and the grandmother. I looked at the lady called my mother who looked half shaken and half fascinated by what was happening. She was as silent an observer as I was. Her fascinated state of mind reminded me of that toy I was fascinated by. She looked as confused about disagreements as I was split between the desire to play or sleep. In a nutshell I realised that the emotion called love was as big a confusion as wanting the opponent to surrender are his ego and agree to disagree over issues with all smile and eyes wide open. With eyes wide open, the confusion cannot persist. In other words with an awaken state of mind love cannot persist. With eyes wide open everything is visible. The good, the bad, the sense of agreement and the extent of disagreement, everything is obvious. If, therefore, I have to grow up till the age and rage of my so called father, I would know for sure that life is all about agreements and disagreements and if still people lived with each other it was born out of the selfish desire of each individual.

The selfish desires of being possessed or a shelter for his/her own emotions. I noticed this dilemma in the mother's eyes. She was unsheltered and seeing the figure called the fathers behaviour towards grandma, I realised he was equally unsheltered. I was full of questions. Can one unsheltered individual act as an umbrella for an equally unsheltered individual? The hunt for me would be futile. One individual heated with emotions cannot protect another heated individual. It would add heat to the previously heated emotions. Each one crying because of the additional heat while the search was initiated for a soothing umbrella.

After sometime I noticed that the figure called a father had a mask on his face, which to my naked eyes looked totally artificial. He had decided, artificially though to cool down for the moment. With his artificiality others seemed to smile. To me that meant that artificiality was important in relationships. When I saw everybody smiling, I knew it was artificiality in totality. The lady called the mother guessed it too. She half smiled. She wanted originality of expressions.

I therefore realised that what is artificial cannot last for a long time. It had its own transparency and the moment the artificiality became transparent there was pain, gloom and lost individuals, completely unsheltered and the path called life goes on and on, each individual protecting himself, yet moving unprotected from the dangers of none other than himself, his own desires, his own emotions for himself... Fearful, painful and analytical of the rest like himself...

From the wrinkles of the grandma her sobbed eyes I realised that the wrinkles came as an effect of the search for self-worth in eyes of others........... continuously.........while passing through the testing time over the long journey.

BEST SELLING TITLES OF GPH

जीवन में पूर्ण स्वास्थ्य प्राप्ति के लिए और सभी बीमारियों से छुटकारा पाने के लिए आज ही पढ़ें।

AVAILABLE IN HINDI ALSO